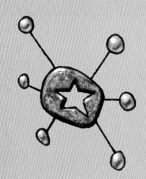

For Rachel, Sally, and Catie
with my love

Published in 2000 in the United States by Ragged Bears, Inc.
413 Sixth Avenue, Brooklyn, New York 11215
www.raggedbears.com

Originally published in Great Britain in 1999 by Ragged Bears Publishing
Milborne Wick, Sherborne, Dorset DT9 4PW

CIP Data is available.

First American edition. Printed and bound in Singapore.

ISBN 1-929927-05-3

2 4 6 8 10 9 7 5 3 1

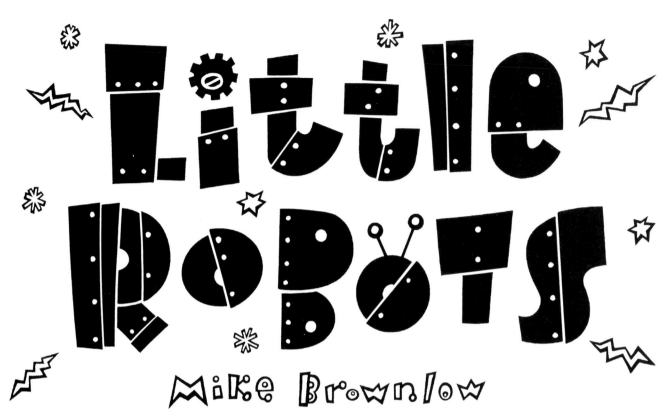

Little Robots

Mike Brownlow

RAGGED BEARS
Brooklyn, New York • Milborne Wick, Dorset

Yellow robot... bright and shiny

Here's his friend who's really tiny

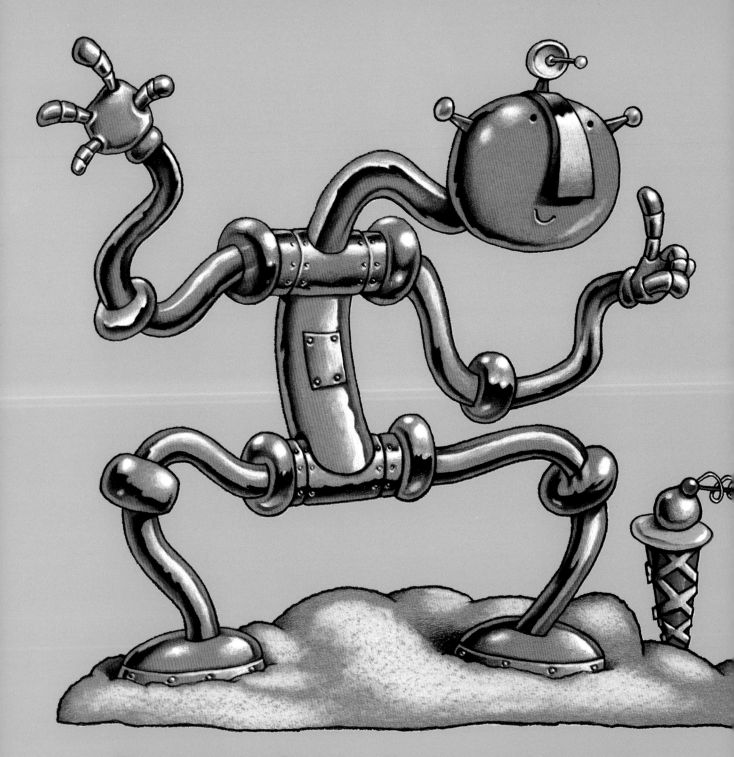

Orange robot... long and bendy

Purple robot... cool and trendy

Spotty robot... round and heavy

Stripy robot loves his teddy

Sporty robot loves to jog

Scruffy robot... messy dog!

Skinny robot... tall and thin

Noisy robot... what a din!

Sparky robots shine their lights

And brighten up the darkest nights

Smiley robot waves at you

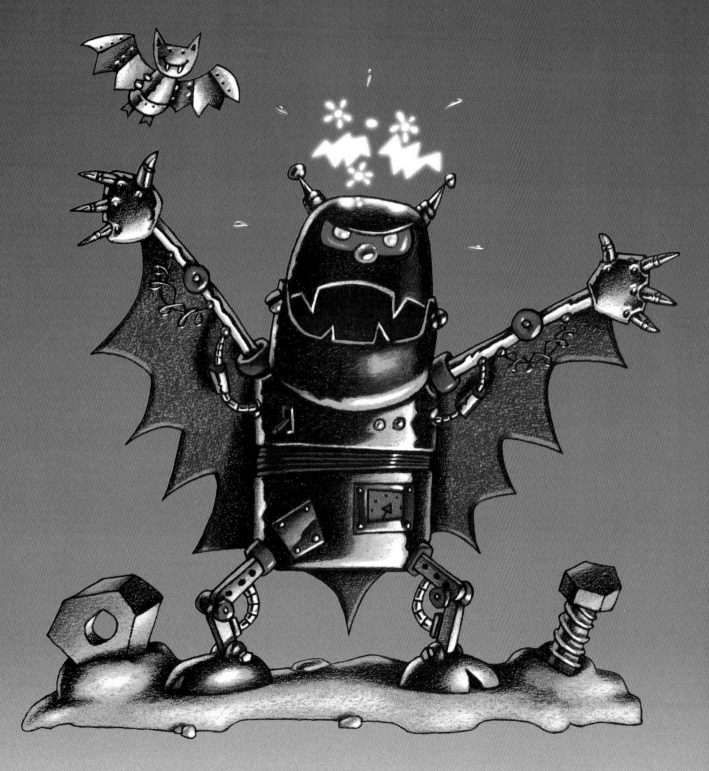

Scary robot shouts out "BOO!"

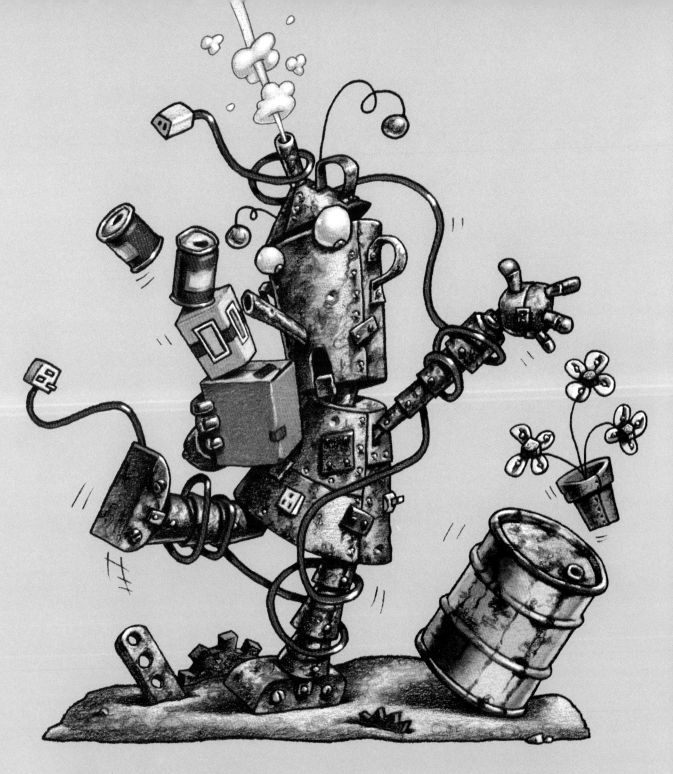

Rusty robot... what a muddle

Tiny robot wants a cuddle

Fluffy robot... pink and frilly

Dopey robot... really silly

Bouncy robot... look out! Thump!

The other robots fall down... Bump!

Little robots dance about

Little robots sing and shout!

Then...
clink clank yawn and bleep bleep bleep

Little robots go to sleep!

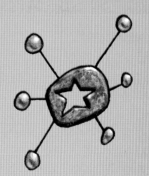